PIRATE'S PLEASURE

CALLED BY A PIRATE BOOK TWO

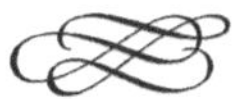

MARIAH STONE

PIRATE'S PLEASURE

A Time Travel Romance

Called by a Pirate series
Book Two

Mariah Stone

CHAPTER 1

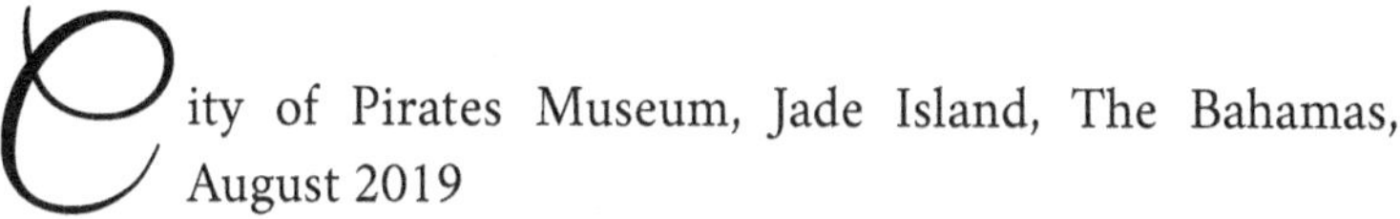

ity of Pirates Museum, Jade Island, The Bahamas, August 2019

Lisa

Cole the Black does something to me. I'm in some sort of trance, watching his onyx eyes under his low eyebrows. Slight stubble covers his strong jaw, and a scar crosses his cheekbone. His hair, long and dark, is held back above the ears in a partial ponytail, the rest reaching past his shoulders. His features are sharp and rough. Dangerous. How can a painting in a frame cause this feeling? Maybe this bedazzlement is what a snake induces in a mouse before launching and eating it alive.

A nudge in my ribs startles me. I shoot a quick glance at Samantha, my best friend, who is standing next to me in the City of Pirates Museum. She studies James "Prince" Barrow's portrait hanging beside Cole's. Between them, two antique jade necklaces hang on the wall.

"He's so handsome." She stares at James. "And yet he couldn't find a date for the ball."

I study James's golden hair and violet eyes, square jaw, and straight nose. He's such a contrast with Cole. James is more the type of man I'm naturally attracted to, the ultimate Prince Charming.

Just like Hank, my ex-fiancé.

"Who wouldn't go to a ball with him, Samantha?" I ask, a knot forming in my throat. "No man can look this dreamy."

The thought of Hank sobers me up and makes my skin ache like an icy shower after a warm bath. He was everything I wanted. My mind buzzes, and my eyes prickle, but tears don't come, courtesy of three piña coladas Samantha poured into me at breakfast.

She rolls her eyes. "I wouldn't." She points at Cole's portrait. "The other guy is my type."

I continue staring at James. It's safer. I'm afraid if I look at Mr. Dangerous again, he'll step out of the portrait, put me over his shoulder and carry me away to do dirty and dangerous things with me. Forbidden pleasures and wild rides. Things good girls like me aren't supposed to want.

"I thought we could spice up our sex life," I remember Hank saying.

"Are you bored with me?" I had asked, mortification dripping down my skin like melting ice.

He looked down. "Frankly, yes, babe. It's all the rules you have. No lights, no oral sex, no—"

He stops talking, sighs, and looks at me. My arms and legs are like wet cotton.

"How about we go to a swing club so that you can experience other pleasures?" he suggests.

"You want to sleep with another woman? You're *that* bored with me?"

The memory twists my stomach and plants a headache

behind my temples. I shake my head and force myself to look at Cole, hoping for a distraction.

Cole is different from Hank. Where Hank is charm itself, Cole is clearly a predator who uses women for his pleasure as if he owns them. He probably dazes them, like me, bends them to his will. Then tosses them away. He's afraid to love, I decide.

Afraid to get hurt.

If only men like him opened up to love, they wouldn't feel the need to sleep with anyone else.

Reminds me of someone I know—Samantha.

"Well, Cole the Black does look like your type, Samantha," I say. "He needs someone to love his lost soul, just like you."

She snorts, but I just smile and shake my head. She deserves the happiness of a lifetime with the right man. And I believe she'll find it.

I believe I will, too, despite Hank. Despite the fact that I'm spending my and Hank's five-year anniversary with Samantha. Despite my broken heart.

I'm loyal, and I was ready to work on our relationship. And he…he just wanted to sleep with other women.

"I can't do that," I'd said.

"Then we are done," he'd said.

And here I am.

Nausea rises in my stomach, and I turn my face to the breeze that brings the scents of pear, mango, and hot stones through the open window. Beyond it, the dark-blue Atlantic shimmers under the sun.

The personal tour guide Samantha hired raises his eyebrows. Adonis is a native to the island and wears a white T-shirt, a bright-red headscarf, a necklace of colorful beads, and a live snake.

"Don't be afraid," Adonis says.

"I'm not," I respond and lean closer to watch the snake slither and stick its tongue in the air.

"Are you crazy? Get away from it," Samantha says.

I smile, enjoying her surprise. She thinks she knows me, but there are things I've never told her. Like about how I've always fantasized that Hank would take me, dominate me, because he couldn't take his next breath otherwise. The reality was that he'd always made me do most of the work and only let me come on rare occasions.

"Are you kidding, Sam?" I say as I study the snake. "I've never had a snake stay in my hotel."

Adonis throws a curious glance at me. "You have a hotel?"

"A pet hotel, in New Jersey." I smile at the snake. "I love animals. I have three dogs and two cats, all from the local shelter. They're with my parents now, and I miss them terribly."

Samantha sighs. "What a brilliant way to use your NYU degree, opening a tiny business in a tiny area and being able to hire no more than two employees. You could be in media like me by now and live in Manhattan. We'd buy two apartments next to each other."

"Ah, stop it, Sam. I love my furry clients, and business is going great."

She rolls her eyes a little bit, and Adonis goes on to tell us about James. Cole and James were friends—both pirates, both captains of their own ships. They'd raided a Spanish treasure ship, but James encountered trouble and had to fight for his life. Cole had ended up with the treasure, with the understanding that should something happen, whoever had the treasure would split it with the other once the waters calmed.

"Cole kept his word and hid James's part of the treasure," Adonis says with a sly smile.

"See," I say. "I told you, Cole was just a lost soul. He could have taken all the treasure for himself, but he didn't. He just needs love to open up his heart."

Samantha shakes her head. "I'm astonished you are still a hopeless romantic even after the breakup."

Adonis chuckles, and it looks like he exchanges a knowing look with the snake. I frown. Did I just imagine that?

He goes on to tell us that the reason James needed a date for the governor's ball was to steal the third clue Cole had left him. He needed a woman to impersonate his wife.

But without that date, James never found the treasure, never settled down as he had wanted to, and once he got back to Bristol, he was hanged for piracy. The story is so sad, it makes my chest tighten.

"I wish he had found a woman who could help him," I say, and Adonis hides a smile.

"Was the treasure found?" Samantha asks.

"Yes. Eventually. These two necklaces"—he points at the space between the portraits—"are their replicas. Two identical necklaces, for two noble twin sisters in Spain. Cole put one in James's half and kept one for himself."

"Why jade?" Samantha asks.

"They say in voodoo, jade is the gem of love, so strong that people are able to find each other anywhere. Even through time."

Samantha and I exchange a look, and I know she finds this ridiculous. While all this talk of finding each other through time and voodoo is not true, I do find the notion of timeless love romantic.

"Would you like to try it on?" Adonis says.

"What?" Samantha says. "Aren't we forbidden from touching stuff in a museum?"

Adonis smiles. "Not when I am your tour guide."

I grin. Samantha brought me here to distract me and to give me an adventure. Well, here we go.

"Yeah!" I say. "Why not. They are replicas anyway, right?"

He removes the necklaces and hands us one each. I jerk a little as a buzz goes through me when the cool metal lands in my palm. It's probably just that I'm so excited—and a little drunk. But the necklace is pretty. The gold is pale and obviously handmade. The sun pattern around the jade stone is as delicate as lace. I've never owned anything jade, but I do like the stone. It's mesmerizing, all those dots and layers, like it represents the whole universe.

"Yes, just replicas," Adonis says. "Put them on. Go on."

"I don't know." Samantha shakes her head and holds the necklace out to Adonis. "What if the guard comes? Aren't we going to get into trouble?"

Adonis winks. "The guard won't come. I promise. When else will you have a chance to try on a pirate treasure?"

Samantha looks at me, I look at her, and we both nod to each other slightly. "All right," Samantha says. "A fun thing to do. Something to remember in New York."

While she puts the necklace on, Adonis and his snake study me. As my eyes lock with the snake's, my head spins a little, and all I can see for a moment is its glittering gaze.

It has jade eyes.

Did I notice that before?

All thoughts evaporate from my head.

"While James was hunting for the treasure, Cole stayed back in the Caribbean," Adonis says. "Unlike James, Cole came from a poor family. But working for years as sailors without pay made them friends. Cole had seen injustice, violence, and poverty since he was a boy. He had a big family in Bristol and worked on a ship to send them money. Because there was no pay in honest labor, Cole became a pirate. Like that, he could support his family."

My heart squeezes, imagining the thin, little dark boy in rags. Even dangerous souls have the reason to be so.

"But as he grew rich and powerful," Adonis says, "he became entangled with—hmm, how shall I say it—unusual sexual interests."

The words drip down my skin like cold water.

"See, I knew there was something like that about him," I mumble.

"Yes, he doesn't want commitment, and he's quite happy in his adventures, especially the ones he has in bed. Or so he thinks. Deep down, I'm afraid he is rolling into the life of a lonely man who has tried everything except for the one thing that will really make him happy."

I swallow. "What is that?"

He winks. "You said it yourself."

My lips part, and a single word escapes my mouth on an exhale. "Love."

He looks at my hands, and I realize I'm still holding the necklace.

"Why don't you try it on?"

I look at Cole's portrait and put the necklace on. It's as though his eyes shift and land on me. Maybe I have heatstroke.

The world trembles. Wind blows from all sides, whistling in my ears. I suddenly remember Samantha has just put on the necklace, as well, and look at her.

But she's not there. What happened? Where is she?

I begin to disappear, as though the wind is blowing me away.

Adonis's voice rings. "You are traveling back in time to help Cole. You wanted to help his lost soul, so here you go. To travel back to modern times, you must put on the necklace."

What sort of craziness is this? The snake's jade eyes are the only thing I see, while the wind is blowing sand against my skin, slowly erasing me.

I must be dreaming. Or something must have been in that piña colada, because everything whirls and twirls and careens like a ship in a storm.

I scream for help, but my voice disappears on the breeze.

And I fall into oblivion.

CHAPTER 2

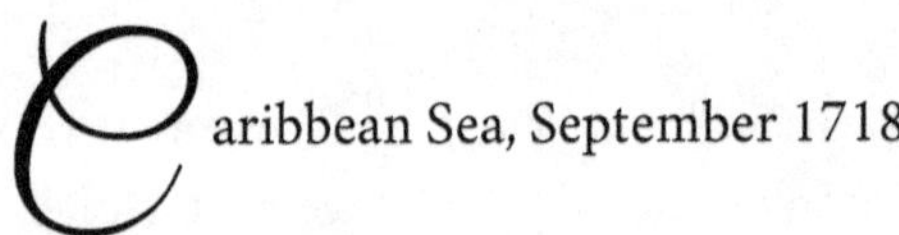

aribbean Sea, September 1718

Lisa

THE SCENT of wood and sea envelops me. The floor sinks under my feet, then rises. Waves splash nearby. Someone groans softly, as if they're being tortured. Did I make that sound? The planks under me scratch my fingers and the bare skin of my legs.

Worry settles in the pit of my stomach. Where am I? Am I dreaming?

I manage to open my eyes, squinting into the golden-orange light of the setting sun that falls through a large window, which is atilt. There's a massive wooden bed, the sheets crumpled and scattered. Against one wall is a desk, and a big chair is half turned with its back to me. Someone is in the chair, and now I know the source of the groan I heard a few seconds ago. They

8

moan again and grunt, moving their hand rhythmically up and down, and I recognize the pungent scent of a man—of sex.

I freeze and hold my breath, all dizziness gone. My face singes. The skin on my chest burns where just a moment ago, a jade necklace hung. My feet weaken and my hands shake. My heart thumps in my ears. I'm in someone's bedroom, they are having sex, and I haven't been invited. The room looks like something out of the past. Am I still in the City of Pirates Museum?

I look around. On the wall by the bed, a riding crop hangs, and above the bed on the ceiling, a mirror. I gasp without a sound.

Oh God, this all seems so real. I feel like a voyeur, observing the man's private moment. I need to get out of here.

I stand up, and now I can see the man clearly.

I should cover my eyes, turn away, let him know he's not alone. But my blood is simmering with excitement. I know I ought to leave, sneak through that closed door and hope he doesn't notice me.

But it's like I'm caught in a trance again.

All I can do is watch, paralyzed, like a mouse waiting for a snake to get me.

He is completely naked, leaning back in the chair. His head is tilted back slightly, his eyes closed. His long, athletic legs are stretched out in front of him and set wide apart. He has massive, sculpted shoulders, glorious pecs I could snowboard over. His long, dark hair is spread across his shoulders and chest. His biceps muscle flexes rhythmically as he pleases himself. The six-pack of his powerful stomach stiffens and glistens with sweat.

My gaze crawls farther down his body to the place where his hands are moving. Heat rushes through me, and I suck in air as I see his length, his thickness. The sight makes the deep muscles within me clench, sending a wave of molten heat through me.

He moves one hand along his erection while the other cups his balls and massages them.

This is so wanton, so dirty. My breath quickens and the space at the apex of my thighs burns. Warmth runs through the lower part of my body, desire licking my nerves. I've never seen Hank do this. I've never seen anyone do this. I even shy away from masturbating myself, afraid someone might walk in and see me.

Oh God, what is wrong with me? I should find Samantha and never drink a piña colada again.

Feeling as though my flip-flops weigh fifty pounds, I tear my feet off the floor and take several wobbly steps towards the door. I skulk, but my traitorous flip-flops slap against my feet.

The man freezes and turns his head.

My gosh… It's Cole the Black…

Or someone who looks exactly like him. His gaze crawls up and down my body, surprised and heavy with desire. In one graceful movement, he's on his feet and a cutlass is clenched in his hand. He's naked and still aroused, his erection big and thick.

I can't move. He walks towards me, his erection swaying slightly. My breath accelerates, and I take a step back, then another.

"What do we have here?" he says when he's so close to me his heavy masculine scent reaches me. He's looming over me like a giant mast, his thin lips spread in a small, sly smile surrounded by rough-looking stubble. "Like what you see, sweetheart?"

Something cold and sharp presses against my neck. He's pointing the cutlass at me. Sweat breaks through my skin, and I open my mouth, but fear grips my throat and the words stick.

"Who are you, beautiful, and how did you get into my cabin without me noticing?"

His voice rumbles, deep and slow and warm but with a

mocking undertone. It reverberates in my chest and undoes the knot in my throat.

Does he really think I'm beautiful? The thought kindles warmth in my whole body.

"I'm not sure how I got here," I say. "I'm sorry, I was just on my way out. I didn't mean any harm. You won't see me again."

He eyes my face slowly, taking in every detail, he half closes his eyelids and tilts his head back. "There is no need to make haste. We just met. I am eager to get better acquainted. But first, I must make sure you did not come to kill me."

"I didn't! I promise."

With one hand still pointing the sword at my throat, his other hand brushes against my side, my waist, his fingers searching. They graze one nipple, then the other, and I gasp and arch into his hand. His touch ignites my skin and melts my muscles, and he only smirks at my reaction. I withdraw, embarrassed at the eagerness of my body. His hand goes down to my shorts and glides against them, going into the back pockets and the front pockets, brushing close to my sex, and I clench, aroused and embarrassed and angry.

Cole then takes my little crossbody purse and opens it with one hand. He retrieves my phone and turns it in his hand with a puzzled look.

"What is this?" he asks.

"It's a phone." I frown. I'm still at the museum, aren't I? And this guy must be an actor or something… He is too convincing, though. He sounds like he's never seen a phone in his life. "You call people with it."

"Oh, like a bell. I doubt you can kill me with this."

He throws it on the floor, and I wince at the loud bang it makes.

Then off go the hotel-room key card, the lipstick, the card holder.

He hesitates when he turns my sunglasses in his hand.

"Clever," he says. "Dark spectacles. Convenient for the Caribbean."

Thank God I left my passport in the hotel room, because everything else flies across the room and onto the floor. He turns the purse over and shakes it. When nothing else comes out, he tosses it to the floor as well.

He narrows his eyes at me, and his cocky smile widens.

"Where did all those objects come from? And your garments? Is it the latest French mode?"

"Not really. And I bought all those in a store like everyone else."

He hums and cocks his head.

"I love puzzles," he says. "And you are one. You come here in your strange undergarments, having all these mysterious objects and watch me please myself. Do you want me to please you, darling? Coming here like a dinner on a plate, ready to be eaten. Would you like me to eat you?"

He says the last bit next to my ear, his warm breath caressing my skin and sending sparks through my blood. My body softens and screams, *yes*! But I haven't lost my mind just yet.

"You're wrong. I didn't come here to do anything with you. I don't know how I got here. All I want is to go back to my friend."

And just as I think about Samantha, I remember the jade necklace, Adonis and the snake, and the voice in my mind hits me so loud, I start. *You are traveling back in time to help Cole.*

And then, *To return to this time, you must put on the necklace.*

A shiver runs through me. Time travel? To Cole? Could it be? No, there must be another explanation.

"You are not going anywhere until I let you." His voice caresses me. "And I am just getting started."

CHAPTER 3

ole

THE LITTLE FEMALE is so delicious, I barely manage to restrain myself. My arms ache to lift her up, let her hook my waist with her legs, and tear apart the tiny blue undergarment that barely hides her arse.

I want her to want me. I've never taken a woman against her will and will not start now, but I crave to plunge into her. I'm still aroused, even though I do not know who she is or why she is here.

She intrigues me. Those big golden eyes the color of rum are intoxicating. The long blond hair looks silky and smooth. That beautiful face, so delicate and soft and feminine...all my instincts scream at me to have her. She looks so pure I want to tempt her, to seduce her, to test if her innocence is an act or genuine. I do not get to play with women like her often. Most of my lovers are experienced—my sexual tastes do not suit virtuous girls.

But this one—

There is something about her I cannot put my finger on. If I'm truthful with myself, I've grown tired of the whores and noblemen's bored wives. One of the reasons I want to go to the East Indies is to savor exotic women. Live new adventures.

But this time, an adventure has walked right into my arms. All fresh and innocent and ripe. Speaking strange words, wearing strange clothes, carrying strange objects in her purse. She is concealing something from me, and I must find out what it is. Did one of my crew send her?

"Are you Cole the Black?" she whispers.

God, her scent spurs my desire to the next level. She smells so clean, like orange and bergamot, sun and sin. She is aroused —was aroused—I could scent her delicious dampness even from here.

"I am," I murmur.

"Do you have the Spanish jade necklace?"

I stiffen and step back, eyeing her carefully, my cutlass still at her throat.

"Why?" I ask.

"I need it to go back. Please."

Her eyes are wide, and she watches me from under her long, thick eyelashes. She looks earnest, but I have seen every trick on this earth from the whores who usually warm my bed.

"What is your name, beautiful?" I ask.

"Lisa."

"Lisa," I say, and even the name is sweet on my tongue. "I understand one of my crew sent you to please me, so naturally you want to make sure you shall get paid. But, darling, you need to work for your pay first. Why do you not undress and get in the bed. As you can see, I am ready for you."

Her eyes widen. "I'm not a prostitute!"

"Forgive me, I did not mean to insult your profession. A courtesan, then. A professional lover. Rest assured, Lisa—Elizabeth, is it?—I have nothing but respect for your line of business. God knows, I am a happy consumer. But just so that we have an understanding, the jade necklace is not on the table."

Her cheeks turn an adorable pink, so pink they rival the color of the sunset. "No!" she says. "I didn't come to have sex with you."

I love when a woman role-plays resistance. Especially as earnestly as she is doing. She is an excellent actress.

"No? Why did you come, then, dressed like a present?"

"I think I traveled back in time. I think—oh God, this sounds ridiculous, I know, but I think I traveled back in time when Adonis made me put that jade necklace on. I was looking at your portrait—yours and your friend James Barrow's. And then Adonis said I need to help you and that I need to wear the necklace again to get back home."

I frown trying to see the sign of a jest. A curl of her lip. A sparkle in her eye. But she looks earnest. A little frightened even. Marvelous performance.

I laugh. "Time travel? You do not expect me to give you the necklace for that nonsense, do you?"

She sighs. "I know, I know. It sounds crazy. God. I don't know what else to do."

Her eyes travel around the room, searching. She must be looking for the necklace. It is in the chest by the bed, locked away safely. Her eyes land on the chest and she frowns. She cannot possibly know it is there, but she might suspect.

God, I want her.

Then an idea strikes me. Since she knows James, is it possible he sent her to amuse me, to play a game with me? A fun challenge for a bored pirate.

I'll make her mine. I'll go along with the theater piece she's playing for me.

"What are you prepared to do to go back home?" I say.

She swallows. "Anything."

I put down my cutlass. "Anything?"

Her eyes widen as she realizes my meaning. She looks me up and down, and I harden again. She takes a step back, paling a little.

"Anything?" I repeat.

"Not anything."

Oh yes, mouse, run and hide. I know all you want is to be taken and seduced and shown the stars. I'll be all too happy to oblige.

"If I told you that the necklace is right here, in this room, and that you could have it if you let me make love to you, what would you say?"

Her breath quickens, her pupils expand, color comes to her neck and chest. "I'd say you've lost your mind if you think I'll sleep with a stranger."

Stranger, she says. She's a little princess then. A good girl. I know every good girl wants to be bad. And I am the bridge from the light to darkness.

"Ah, so you need an intimate connection," I say. "You want to get to know me better. You want to trust the person you sleep with. You want to feel valued and special. Am I correct?"

Her eyebrows crawl together and pain flickers through her face. I scratched right where it itched.

"You can trust me, that while you're mine, I won't let any harm come to you. While you're mine, I'll make your body sing. While you're mine, you'll be the queen, and my only purpose in life will be to please you. That you can trust. I'll make you mine, and you'll love it."

I see her pink lips part, swell a little and darken. She's aroused. She likes what she hears.

Good.

"And you can also trust that this arrangement has an ending, and as soon as you leave my sight, I shall forget about you."

I watch her eyes widen and the inner edges of her eyebrows crawl up.

"This is what you can expect and trust. And while you're mine, I expect full submission. You say yes to whatever I want to do with you. But rest assured, it won't be anything you can't take."

Her cheeks flush. She studies me, thinking. I know she wants me. I know she's tempted. I just need to push her a little. And she shall fall into my hands.

"Are you married?" I ask.

Her face stiffens, and an expression of hurt flees across it. I think I know what pains her. The ache of a broken heart, of rejection. The pain I knew all too well since Duchess Chestwitch.

"No," she says.

"A lover?"

She shakes her head.

"Come on, darling. Have this adventure. Let me open new frontiers of pleasure for you. Let me show you what your body was designed to do and feel. Tomorrow you will be back in your normal life. Tonight, experience a pirate's pleasure. You give yourself to me just for tonight, and I shall give you the necklace."

She studies me, her eyes like bronze in the semidarkness of the waning sunset. As the last of the sunrays disappear from the opposite wall, Lisa straightens her shoulders and lifts her chin. Her eyes harden with a decision.

"And I get to ask you three questions no one has ever asked you. And you get to tell me things you haven't told anyone."

My jaw tightens. I am a private man. I am liberal with my body but not my soul. There are things about me not even James knows. Her final condition might be too much.

But I study her, her golden sweetness, her unusual clothing. I have never met anyone like her. And never will again, I somehow know. I will answer her questions. How bad can they be?

"And the questions," I agree.

She nods. "All right, Cole. It's time I do this crazy thing I've wanted to do for a long time. My fiancé didn't like it, but maybe you're a better man for it. But also, I know there's hope even for you. I don't believe you just want to move from one woman to the next. I'll show you there's more to you than just sex. So, I will ask you the three questions. You will give me the necklace. And in exchange, I will"—she swallows—"give myself to you, under your terms. What do you say? Three questions and me for the necklace?"

"I agree, madame."

She nods, her golden eyes as hard as amber. "But know this, Cole the Black. Neither of us wakes up tomorrow morning the same person. I'm ready. Are you?"

CHAPTER 4

 isa

"I AM READY, DARLING," Cole purrs.

Oh God! My stomach clenches and jumps into my throat as if I'm on a roller coaster just before the deepest plunge of my life.

He puts the sword on the chest of drawers and brushes my cheek with his knuckles. The touch glides like silk against me, electrifying my skin. The hair on the back of my neck stands up. My head is light, and as a wave hits the ship, I lose my balance. Cole catches me by the elbows and steadies me, and he's so close to me I can feel the heat of his body even through my top. He watches my lips so intently, as though they pain him. Then he lowers his head and kisses me.

I should step back. I should protest and stand up for myself. I should take his sword and put it at his throat and demand the necklace.

But I can't. I want this kiss too much. Something deep within me craves the taste of his darkness.

When his teeth gently nip my lip, I know there will be no way back.

Because the poison of dark desire tastes too good.

His kiss is so tender, I'm taken by surprise. I thought he'd be powerful and demanding. Maybe even rough.

But his lips are so soft, all of my nerve endings wake up and reach for him, intoxicated. His taste, the barely noticeable whiff of rum on his breath, the scent of his sun-kissed skin, and the tang of virile male send fire roaring through my veins.

I respond. My lips press back against his, gently as well, and we freeze for a moment, swimming in the sensation. He withdraws a little, and I sway, lost without him. He stands a step away from me and devours me with his eyes.

"What are you doing to me?" he growls, and crushes me against his hard, naked chest. He kisses me again, hungry now, desperate. I respond and our tongues lash in a wild dance. He engulfs me, his arms around me like a warm vise. He runs them down my waist and grabs my behind and squeezes. A satisfied moan escapes his throat. He moves his hands under my butt and lifts me up. I envelop his waist with my legs.

My head spins as he carries me somewhere. I'm warm wax, heated by his arms, ready to be sculpted and be made into whatever he wants. I've never felt so desired, never been so turned on in my life.

He puts me on the bed and covers me with his body. His weight is pleasant on me. His cock is pressing against my sex, my clothes the only thing between us, and I instinctively tighten my legs around him and crush him into my body. His mouth is so skillful, I think maybe he can make me come just by kissing me.

I moan, writhing under him.

God, I never felt like this with Hank.

Hank...

I open my eyes to stare right at my reflection, covered by Cole's sculpted body. His round, perfect ass clenches rhythmically as he rubs his pelvis against me.

This is not me. I'm a good girl. Good girls are unworthy if they're promiscuous... The words engraved in my memory by Mother pound in my temples. I remember the first time it happened. I was thirteen and we came back from church with our neighbors. Paul, the boy I liked, kissed me in the backyard. Mom saw us, and with red cheeks, her eyes bulging, she came at us. "You are a good girl!" she'd yelled. "No man will love you if you behave like this! You won't be worth anything to a man if you're promiscuous."

Cole hugs me, and in one swift movement he turns me around so that I'm on top.

"I want to see your gorgeous arse as I'm about to take you," he murmurs and opens his eyes, looking behind me.

At the mirror, I realize.

I freeze, the memory of Hank's words, the hot, biting embarrassment burning my whole body. I want to cover myself, to hide somewhere safe, somewhere no man can ridicule me.

"Having sex with a blow-up doll is hotter." Hank's words pound in my head. "It's over."

A headache is born in my skull as the memories of rejection, embarrassment, and humiliation flood my psyche.

I'm not ready to go through the same again.

Cole is watching me, his eyes still, dark pools of desire. He's panting.

"What is it?" he says.

I slide to the side and sit on the bed, hugging my knees. "I'm sorry."

"Why?"

He's not disgusted. He's not shocked. He's not rejecting me. On the contrary, his handsome face reflects concern and care.

"I'm not good at this. At this sex thing."

Cole sits up, his onyx eyes glare.

"Who told you that?" Cole growls.

"Hank. My ex-fiancé."

Cole's fists clench, his eyes harden. He cups my jaw. "He has no notion what he is talking about. Just your kiss made me want to rip your silly garment apart."

Heat flushes through me. Is he right? Could Hank be wrong? Suddenly, I want nothing more than to prove Hank wrong—no, to prove myself wrong. To show myself that a real, kinky pirate is turned on by me.

Our eyes lock, and all the breath is sucked out of my lungs.

"How did you first fall in love?" I say to distract him. "That's question number one."

His lips press into a thin line, his eyes darkening. "She was a passenger on the ship I served on. She was older than me. I was just a boy. She taught me things—many things. About my body, about the art of submission and domination. About the art of patience. And the limits between pain and pleasure that can be stretched and pushed. She—" He sat in silence for a while before continuing. "She made me who I am. This is how I fell in love. Through my body."

I imagine a small cabin in a ship, Cole—young and dark-eyed—with an older woman tying his hands. The image makes me sick. I stretch my arm to him and cup his jaw. His eyes darken even more, and he just opens his mouth to say something when a knock sounds at the door. A middle-aged man with bushy sideburns sticks his head into the room.

"Cap'n, a ship on the horizon, south-southwest. Heading right at us. Can't see what he's flying."

Cole frowns. "I'm coming, Jenkins."

Jenkins disappears, but Cole calls after him, "Did you employ Lisa?"

I gasp, angry. Did we not just establish that I wasn't a whore? Jenkins ogles me. "I do not think I had the pleasure."

Cole frowns and stands up, finds his trousers and puts them on. "Someone else, then?"

"Not that I know of."

"Told you!" I cry out. "I traveled through time."

Cole pulls on his shirt, then his boots, without taking his eyes off me.

"We shall see. Stay here while I'm dealing with the ship."

isa

I SIT for a moment and stare at the door behind which Cole disappeared. A ship is following us? Are we in danger?

I stand up and walk to the window, and even I can see the silhouette of a ship on the horizon—three rows of sails, black against the glowing orange and red of the dying sunset. What adventure had Adonis sent me on?

Speaking of which, the necklace is still here somewhere, and I'm alone. My hands shake a little. Will he be gone long?

I must look for it. But where do I start?

The massive desk is littered with books and maps. There's a quill in a little ink jar and an abacus. One book is open, and there's a sort of table where names are written next to a list of loot, along with who got what share. The table looks clean and precise, and it's clear payments were made directly after the raids. Cole is a fair captain, it seems.

My heart warms at the thought. He's a kind man, I knew it.

I go through the desk drawers and find boxes with gunpowder, guns, knives. In one there's an old Bible and a small wooden cross on a simple string. I take it in my hands and turn it over. There's an engraving that reads, "To Cole from Mother" and a small heap of folded envelopes with the same address on them: Blackwood Family, Water Lane, Bristol.

All sealed. None sent.

I brush my fingers against Cole's sharp, precise handwriting. My heart squeezes at the thought that he must be missing his family if he wrote to them, if he still sends them support.

He has a soul, and a heart.

My chest fills with lightness, my stomach with the fluttering wings of hummingbirds. Oh no. I'm starting to feel more than I'm supposed to. I'm about to leave him. Now is not the time to fall for a pirate from another century!

I need to find the necklace. I shut the drawer, turn and bump something with my hand. A dark object flies through the air, falls on the floor and shatters, spilling black ink everywhere.

I freeze, and an angry bird's squawks fill the room. I look in the far corner and see a tall iron cage partly covered with a white sheet. No, no, no, someone will hear it. I dash there and lift the sheet up.

It's a large green parrot with bright-yellow feathers around its beak. One wing is clearly broken because it hangs at an awkward angle. Although the break healed, and the bird can lead a good life as a pet, it would never have survived in the wild this way.

"Shhh." I put my finger to my lips. "Please, sweetie, go to sleep. I'm sorry I woke you up."

But it continues to squawk, and I look around helplessly. "Chut, Chut, Chut," the parrot squawks. "Chut up."

I stare at it. "Did you just tell me to shut up?"

"Chut up."

A smile spreads across my lips. A talking parrot. I've had a couple of cockatiels, the miniature cockatoos, stay in my hotel over the last few years, so I know how to deal with birds. I think this is an Amazon parrot, one of the most talkative.

"Okay, okay," I say. "Shutting up."

I continue watching the bird, and it calms down and studies me. It's very pretty and cute. And I can't believe Cole taught it to speak. Or did he buy it like this? Curiosity burns me. A pirate and a parrot. I wonder if the bird likes to sit on Cole's shoulder.

"What's your name?" I ask.

"Cap'n Bluebeard. Cap'n Bluebeard. Oh, blow the man down, bullies, blow the man down," it sings, and I recognize the famous pirate chantey I heard in the museum. "Way aye blow the man down…"

I clasp my hands on my chest in awe.

"Oh, blow the man down, bullies, blow him away," it goes on. "Give me some time to blow the man down!…"

"Oh my goodness, did Cole teach you that?"

"Cole da Black." Captain Bluebeard scratches his beak with his foot.

"Aren't you clever, Cap'n Bluebeard. Well done. Okay, go to sleep now. You didn't see anything." I take the sheet to cover the cage. "I need to keep searching for the treasure."

"Treasure," he says. "Chut up."

I stop and look at the bird. "Do you know where it is?"

"Treasure. Chest. Oh, blow the man down, bullies…"

I look at the wall by the desk, and there are several chests of different sizes. I walk to the first, my hands shaking as I open it. Clothes, furs, textiles. The scent from the second one hits me in the face, an explosion of spices and exotic aromas. There are bottles of rum, little purses and jars with spices, tea, coffee, bottles with oil, and pieces of sandalwood along with other aromatic woods I don't recognize.

"Treasure," Captain Bluebeard says. "Chest."

"Okay, this is treasure, but it's not the one I'm after. I need a jade necklace."

I go to the next chest, but that one is locked. The chest standing next to it is, too. I look around for the key but can't see anything.

"Captain Bluebeard? Where are the keys?"

"Treasure. Chut up."

"The keys. Do you know?"

"Chut. Up. Up. Up."

I frown and look up. There's nothing but the mirror attached to the ceiling.

"Up?" I say.

"Up," he confirms and looks at the mirror as well.

"Oh!" I get on the bed, stand up, and look closer at the mirror. There's a gap between it and the ceiling. I gasp. I'm not tall enough to see what's in the gap, but I reach up and run my hand along the back of the mirror. It's big and rectangular and uneven. I search one side—nothing. The other side—nothing. Then, on the third side, my hand encounters something metal— a bunch of keys. My pulse drumming in my ears, I pull, but they don't move. They must be stuck on something. I move them around, rattle them, but they won't come loose. I feel with the other hand and find a hook. It feels like a complete circle, except there's a tiny gap. I push the key ring through the gap and pull the keys free.

Not believing my luck, I jump off the bed and do a happy dance.

"Okay, maybe it's too early for that. I have no idea if the key is going to fit."

"Treasure," Captain Bluebeard says.

"Yes, treasure." I sink to the chest and try the keys. Finally, after several nerve-racking attempts, it opens.

I gasp again.

What I see there isn't treasure. There are flogs, birch

switches, harnesses, wooden dildos, a string with quite large wooden balls… I shut the lid as though a disease is about to jump out at me. My cheeks burn, and my body heat spikes. My breath rushing in and out, I quickly turn the key and close the lid, but my mind fills with images of Cole using all those things. On me. My nipples harden, my breasts swell, my inner muscles clench in sweet anticipation.

Oh God. Do I like kink?

I turn to Captain Bluebeard. "I hope you didn't mean that this was the treasure."

"Treasure. Oh, blow the man down, bullies, blow him away…"

"You need to learn a new repertoire, my friend."

I move to the next chest and pray I won't find more of those things. A couple of minutes more of fiddling with the keys, and finally I unlock it. When I lift the lid, my breath catches. Treasure. The chest is only half full, but there are gold and silver coins, pearls, gemstones, earrings, necklaces… The jade necklace.

I can go home.

I am still as a statue, looking at it, not believing that I'm really seeing it. Then slowly, as though afraid to spook it, I take it in my hands. It buzzes slightly, just like the one I held back at the museum. And somehow I know it'll work.

Am I ready? Just put it on, and I'll never need to see Cole again. No mirrors, no kink, no riding crops, no talking parrots. No ships chasing us.

Us. My stomach drops.

I don't want to leave Cole yet. I actually want to stay and spend time with him and experience this ride—the wildest ride of my life, I'm sure. And to show to myself that I'm not boring in bed.

Because I've had enough. Enough of following the rules and

being a good girl. It's time to be naughty. And there's no better person to be bad with than Cole the Black.

I return the necklace, lock the chest, and spin around to put the keys back behind the mirror.

But a tall dark figure at the door makes me stop breathing.

"What did you do?" Cole's eyes are a black storm, and its fury is focused on me.

ole

RAGE THUNDERS in me as I watch her sorry face. Lisa is holding the keys to my chests. She is asking to be punished, is she not? She does not reply to my question, just gapes at me.

"What. Did. You. Do?" I say, barely stopping myself from taking her by the shoulders and shaking the answer out of her.

But it's Captain Bluebeard that answers. "Treasure," he says. "Chut up."

"Ah, the secret treasure. I can certainly see that *you* did not help." I throw an angry glance at him.

"I-I'm sorry, Cole," Lisa says. "I did look for the necklace, but I didn't take it."

I cross the distance between us and take the keys from her, then put them on my belt.

"Forgive me, humble lady, but I have lost the ability to believe you," I say, looking around. She broke my ink jar, and the black stain spreads across the floor with the rocking of the ship. "You dishonored our agreement. You will pay for this."

She swallows and pales a little.

"But I didn't dishonor our agreement. I didn't put the necklace on."

She is right. Despite her misconduct with the necklace, she did not put it on and disappear, although she could have. I walk to her and study her beautiful face, her eyes amber in the warm light of the candles. I still do not believe her ridiculous story of time travel, but I do wonder how she got on board. Did she sneak aboard last night when we were docked in Nassau? Does the ship pursuing us aim to retrieve her and the necklace? Why did she not take it?

"Why did you stay, then?"

Her mouth opens slightly. We are so close I can smell her delicious scent. A few more inches and I can claim her mouth.

"Because..." she says. "You still owe me the answers to two questions."

"You seductive vixen," I rumble and kiss her, unable to resist her proximity. It is as though she is the coast and I am a wave, and I have no other option but to crash into her.

She meets my mouth readily, willingly. Her hunger demands me as much as mine demands her. I sink into the delicious warmth of her mouth, kissing, probing, taking. I'm already hard, and I know if I continue for another minute, I won't be able to stop.

And I need to find the spyglass. I need to command the ship now that we seem to be under pursuit. I stop and put my forehead against hers, breathing deeply to regain my senses.

"Did you find anything else besides the treasure?" I ask.

I lean back and see her already flushed face redden even further.

"I found...other stuff," she admits.

"Anything you liked? Anything you wanted to try?"

She inhales sharply, her lips swelling a little.

"There was a bottle of rum that looked good," she says.

I growl a little. "I do not mean rum. And you are perfectly aware of it."

She's quiet and bites her lower lip.

"No matter, darling." I turn and walk to the table. "You already answered with your expression. I intend to try all of what you've seen on you, and you will love it."

I open one of the drawers where my nautical instruments lie. There it is, the spyglass I keep for extreme situations like this.

"Lo and behold, you did not steal or break my spyglass." I take it in my hand. "We might have a chance yet."

"Where did you find Captain Bluebeard?" she asks.

I turn to her and raise one brow. "He was on one of the ships we raided. The poor bastard had his wing broken, so it was either toss him into the sea or take him on. He is the best entertainment on the ship, sings us shanties. The crew is quite fond of him. Has a good voice."

She smiles. "He does. You're very kind to him."

I shrug one shoulder. "I have done little. I only let him stay, that is all."

"And what about those letters," she says. "Why did you never send them?"

Anger rises in me like a wave in a storm. "Did you go through my personal correspondence?"

"No. I just saw them. I didn't read them, of course. I just saw the address on them."

"No one gave you permission to look through my possessions."

"This is the second question, Cole. Remember, I stayed for this. Answer me. Why did you never send those letters to your family?"

My fist clenches so tightly around the metal tube of the spyglass, I am afraid it might break. I forcefully relax my fingers.

She could not ask a worse question—there is no question I want to answer less than this one.

"Why, Cole?" she presses.

Oh, little minx.

"Because my mother had twelve children when I left. My father was a shadow of a man. I did not want to burden them with yet another duty, to spend time reading my letters. Because once they read them, they might feel they need to protect their pirate son from the British Empire. There is a price on my head. What if someone came to them and tried to find out something about me? Worse—what if they couldn't avoid telling my pursuers the truth? My mother would never forgive herself, nor would my father."

Her eyes widen and dampen with tears. Is she feeling for me?

The thought is more disturbing than her question. No. All women want from me is physical pleasure. Cole the Black, who can satisfy a woman's most forbidden desires. That is all I am good for. That is what Duchess Chestwitch showed me.

The whole reason I chose piracy was to avoid becoming a shell of a man, like my father. Hard labor to provide for twelve children and a wife, no matter how much he loved them, was what had made him like that. That is why I do not want to love. That is why I do not want a woman to be responsible for. Because I will either end up like my father or she will use me up and toss me aside as Duchess Chestwitch did.

The spyglass in one hand, I grab Lisa with the other and drag her outside after me. "You've asked me enough questions. Distracted me enough. I must get a better look at the ship pursuing us, and I do not trust you. You will come with me."

"Wait, what? Come where?"

"To the crow's nest."

She struggles and makes me stop. "No! Cole, please. I'm afraid of heights."

I turn her to face me and look into her eyes. "I cannot allow you to stay here alone, and I cannot leave you with my men because you look like a freshly cooked dinner. I will not let harm come to you. This is your fault, my darling. Had you kept your word, I'd have more faith in you. But I should have never trusted you in the first place."

* * *

Lisa

WHEN WE WALK OUT of the cabin, it's already dark. The sky is full of stars that are scattered like tiny snowflakes. The scent of sunbaked wood, tar, and sea envelops me. Then male sweat and rum.

Oh, the deck is real. And those men barking commands, tugging the ropes, and manning the sails are real. I look for the electric lights of a city on the coast, but everything around us is black, except for the stars, and the moon, which shines brightly and casts a glimmering road across the ocean towards the horizon.

Above us, white sails flap on a weak breeze.

Everything looks so real, and I abandon any tiny lingering doubt that I've traveled back in time. As I walk among the sailors, they follow me—curious, hungry, surprised, dangerous... A wave of prickles goes through my hands and arms. It looks like I'm the only woman on a ship full of pirates, and suddenly my tiny denim shorts and transparent T-shirt feel indecent, like I'm not wearing anything at all.

And then Cole stops in front of the tallest mast and looks up. There, in the darkness, on the very top, is the circular little platform.

"Up there, Lisa. Climb."

CHAPTER 7

isa

THE DECK SEEMS SO FAR below us, dark but for the places where torches shine against the night. There, I can see some of the men looking up at us, openly curious. The sight makes my stomach jump and tighten, excitement and fear mixing in a sharp cocktail. We are so high, on this tiny round wooden platform, and the gaps between the planks beneath our feet and the grate-like railing around us—make it feel even more precarious.

"You can't be serious, Cole." My voice comes out tight and high. "Let me go down, please."

"I am dead serious." He stands directly behind me, looking into his spyglass, which is like a little telescope. I feel his hard muscles against my skin, the material of his breeches against my bare legs. I inhale deeply and close my eyes, desire and terror coursing through me in equal measures.

"Union Jack!" Cole yells. "Full spread ahead! East-northeast."

His voice carries the words easily despite the flapping sails and crashing waves. The sailors relay his command and return to manning the ship with even more intense activity. Underneath the sails, standing on the deck, is Jenkins, and he commands the sailors who begin to pull the ropes, moving the sails.

Cole looks again at the ship, then cries, "Ten miles!"

"The bastard's faster than us. Damnation," he mutters.

The ship moves, the crow's nest sinks and rises. The rolling is harsher now, and my stomach jumps to my throat.

"Did you say Union Jack? The British Navy?" I ask.

He turns me to him and looms over me, all dark and mighty in the night. Above us, the stars. Below us, the sea and the ship. Around us, the sails. And he is still the sight that steals my breath away and turns my knees to jelly. "Someone who is flying their flag, at least."

He brushes his knuckles against my cheek. "You are so beautiful. So innocent. So pure."

My mouth dries. He pushes me slightly and presses me against the railing of the crow's nest. "We're about to sail at full speed, chased by the enemy. How do you feel about that?"

He runs one hand down my chest and over my breast, caressing it through the fabric, playing with my nipple until it hardens. I gasp for breath, helpless, as exquisite pleasure spreads through my body. "I'm not sure..." I say. "Like on a really tall roller coaster?"

He lifts me up and sits me on the railing. I shudder and look down, my head spinning from the sight. He wraps his arms around my waist and kisses me. His lips are demanding and yet soft at the same time. His tongue explores my mouth, and it's so delicious my panties grow damp.

"Do you feel alive?" he asks. "When the danger is so near, does it not set all your skin ablaze and make your hair stand up?

Does it not make you feel deeper, hear clearer, and see more colors?"

I lick my lips. "You certainly do, Cole. You do all those things to me. And more."

He growls in his throat and crushes his lips to my mouth.

The ship turns and dips, and we dip with it. The arousal from his touches and the turbulence of the world around us—the naked danger, the swarming activity of the ship, the darkness of the night, and the brilliance of the stars and moon—it is all caressing me. It is all making love to me.

Not just Cole.

And I'm somewhere in a different world, on the other side of the mirror, like Alice. In a world where all of my misgivings and flaws have become bare and open, and all I can do is let them out.

And if I fall and die, that would be a good death because I'd die daring. I'd die living a full life—for the first time ever.

I kiss him back, drunk with excitement and burning with arousal. He removes my T-shirt, and my bikini top, and the wind slaps against my bare skin like a cat-o'-nine-tails, adding fire to my blood. I tug at his shirt, too, and he removes it willingly. His bare chest glides against mine, silky and crisp where he has a little dark hair.

He stops the kiss and whispers against my lips, "Open this devilish lock on your garment."

I smile and jump down to the floor of the crow's nest. I undo the button and the zipper, and he tugs the shorts down my legs, together with the panties. I look around, suddenly aware that any of those sailors who have the right angle can see me like this, completely naked. And how many of them are on the ship —a hundred? More?

The heat of embarrassment floods over me, the urge to cover myself making my hands jerk to my breasts and my crotch. But Cole catches my hands.

"No," he says softly, his eyes two dark pools of sin. "Embrace it. Make love to it. Let it wash through you."

My insides clench, and sweat covers my skin. I want to hide, but there's something so freeing about being exposed like this. There's nowhere to go. Take me or leave me.

"You are perfection," Cole murmurs as his eyes crawl down my body, taking in every detail. "*My* perfection."

He grabs the end of a rope that is hanging from somewhere farther up the mast, then takes my wrists and ties them. My jaw drops open, and I watch in astonishment as he does this, my breath catching in my throat. My whole body tingles. Am I really about to let him—

He pulls another rope and my wrists fly up.

I gasp and jerk my arms, but Cole has already tied the other end of the rope to a hook on the crow's nest.

I'm completely at his mercy. I feel—helpless. Exposed. Beautiful.

Desired.

My breasts rise and fall fast, my nipples harden under Cole's gaze.

He comes to me, and without touching me with his hands, he kisses me. The kiss is gentle and rough at the same time. Possessive.

When I'm completely breathless, he holds my waist and kisses my chin, then trails his lips down my neck and takes one breast in his mouth. I quiver at the heat of his tongue compared to the chill of the air. He cups the other breast with his hand and rolls my nipple between his thumb and index finger, his mouth teasing, tasting, his tongue licking, his hand massaging.

Heat rushes through me, pleasure jolting to the very core of me, making me clench and burn. My head falls back, and I arch into his sweet torture. I want to run my fingers through his hair, I want to dig my nails into his shoulders and bring him closer, make him suck harder. He goes to the second breast and repeats the process, and if not for the ropes holding me, I would fall.

That is when he gets down on his knees, leaving a hot trail of kisses down my belly. With each kiss, I clench, anticipation of where his mouth is heading quickening my breath.

He kisses me all the way down to a small triangle of hair, courtesy of a tasteful bikini wax. When Cole separates my flesh with two fingers and seals his mouth over my sex, all thoughts of who might be watching, of how high we are above the deck, of anything else in the world, evaporate.

His tongue explores me in a circular motion, round and round the clitoris as though he's having an hors d'oeuvre before the main dish, sending all my senses into a melting, beautiful, wonderful mixture of sensations and bursts of pleasure.

And then he hits the epicenter. I moan, arch and put one leg on his shoulder to give him all the access he can get, and he continues, licking, sucking, playing, teasing until I'm about to fall apart around him. Then he withdraws. I sway, helpless with yearning.

A cool breeze kisses me right there, and an eternity of stars is staring at me, lovingly, and the sea whispers sweet nothings. The rope holds me in place, and I realize I'm the yin, there to complement the yang.

There to complement Cole.

And I know he can't exist without me. In my submission is power, and in his domination is weakness.

He grabs my thighs and turns me around so that I face the bow of the ship. Before me is the front mast, the powerful sails, and sailors working below. Anyone could see me at any moment.

I close my eyes and embrace the feeling of exposure as Cole told me to. His warm, callused hands run down my spine, spilling heat as they go. They find the top of my butt, and he runs them around the cheeks, then slaps them playfully. I arch, pushing my butt back into his hands. Then comes another slap, harder. And another, harder. They burn, but in a good way, and I spread my legs.

I feel Cole suck in a breath and fiddle with his trousers, then something hot and hard and long brushes against my butt.

Oh.

The darkness. The freedom. The permission to play bad. To color outside the lines.

To be me.

That's what he's giving me.

And it feels like I'm a sail and he's the wind, and he fills me and gives me direction and purpose.

And then he enters my sleek sex, and the world explodes in all sensations of pleasure. There's the sweetness of chocolate and the bite of rum and the softness of whipped cream. There's the relaxation of a massage and the tightness in the chest before a big jump, and the pleasure of listening to really good salsa music.

And yet, none of these compare to the storm he unleashes inside me. I melt and tighten around him as he begins thrusting into me. He's big—giant—and he stretches me to the limit, then thrusts so deep it hurts.

And I love it. I push my behind back, eager to meet his thrusts. He holds my breasts, then runs his hands down, fingers parting my cleft. His chest presses to my back, his muscles hard and powerful as he continues taking me higher, to the heights of pleasure I've never known.

With his finger, he circles my clit, and I'm dissolving into him. I'm not sure anymore if I'm still me, or if I'm part of him or this ship or the sea.

Maybe I'm everything.

The pressure continues building and building. And then, without warning, I'm falling apart. I'm exploding, shaking, sinking and rising. He shakes, sinking and rising with me. The air fills with his groans as he cries my name and I cry his. I lose the last threat of separation between me and the stars and Cole and the sea.

I'm everywhere.

I'm everything.

I'm seen.

And I see him.

CHAPTER 8

ole

MINE. Mine. She's mine. My heart beats against Lisa's back.

I hold her, still shaking and breathing heavily. She's silky and warm, and we breathe together like one being, the movements of the ship underneath us echoing the rhythm.

I allow myself a moment or two more to absorb the delicacy of her body against mine and flow in the waves of softness. Then I detach myself, untie the rope around Lisa's wrists, and begin to dress.

The experience with her was the most intense I have ever gone through. My time with Duchess Chestwitch does not even compare to the exquisite pleasure I felt with Lisa.

The fresh sea breeze touches my skin, and a cold shiver runs through my body. What I felt with Lisa was so full of light. She took me high, so high I could see the stars and the moon. I worshiped her, as though she was healing water and I was a deathly sick man.

And what I tasted was life.

And I want more.

But there will be no more. She is about to leave me forever.

And I do not want her to stay—why would I? She makes me crave dangerous things. To forget about other women, to want no one but her in my arms for the rest of eternity.

Is what I feel towards her something my father felt towards my mother? I remember the last time I saw him. I was just a boy, getting ready for my first big voyage. His face was too old for his thirty-five years: weathered, wrinkled, tanned like leather. I remember his hunched back, the gray, watery eyes. He always smelled like fish, even after the monthly bathing when my mother scrubbed him clean with lye soap.

"You were born to the wrong family, son," he had said while we were out fishing on his boat—the most precious thing he owned. "Had I never had you, had I never married your mother, I would be free. But you will end up like me." He looked at me and my three older brothers, his face bitter. "You all will. You will all find a girl you will be stupid enough to fall in love with, marry her, and then every year there will be one more mouth to feed. Mark my words."

That was the day I knew I would do everything not to end up like my father. No mouths to feed. No woman to love. No one to tie me down.

These thoughts, these emotions make a cold sweat break through my skin. I haven't loved anyone since Duchess Chestwitch. I was ready to forget my father's prediction. When she got rid of me like of an old undergarment, it almost destroyed me. Although later I realized it meant that I was still free. What I feel now, for Lisa, is so much stronger.

It could make me forget my wish to stay free.

It could ruin my soul completely.

I need to keep my distance from her. She will not stay for

me. I should have never seduced her. But how could I have known that she would taste so good I could not stop?

My chest is tight, my body still aching softly, I refuse to look at her.

"Let us go down. I got distracted, but I am the captain and I have urgent matters on my hands."

Her eyes land on me, heavy and wide. Her pain stabs me in the abdomen. But this is for the best. For both of us.

"Did you not feel what I felt?" she says, and it breaks my heart.

"Get dressed. Let us go down."

She runs her hands through her hair and briefly closes her eyes, then gets up and puts on her small garments.

"Stop being so bossy. Why can't you just talk to me about this?" she asks. "This has been the most transcendent night of my life. You...you are the most amazing—"

Her words tear me apart. "Please, Lisa. No."

Her eyes fill with tears. "Why not?"

These feelings are an illusion. If I give in, if I allow myself one more step towards her, my heart will fill with her. And when she leaves me, she will crush it into dust.

"I felt such a connection with you," she says. "It was magical. Didn't you feel it?"

"There is nothing magical about this, Lisa. I took you on top of the ship, while my sailors could see you. It was a rush of danger combined with skilled lovemaking. That is what you felt. Not magic. Not transcendence. Just good sex."

I turn around and begin the climb down. "Come."

* * *

Lisa

. . .

As soon as we reach the deck, he turns his back to me and walks away, his white shirt flapping on his broad shoulders. I ignore the curious stares of the seamen as well as the question in my head that asks if they are looking because they saw me up there during the most intimate moment of my life or because my clothes make me look like a prostitute in this era. Before, such thoughts would have brought heat to my cheeks. Now, I don't care.

I grab Cole by the arm and turn him around to face me.

"No. You will not walk away from me."

He turns and looks at me, his face pained, his eyes dark. Then he blinks and the expression is gone, replaced by a dark look from under his frowning eyebrows.

I swallow. I will not be intimidated anymore. "That was the deepest emotional and physical connection I've ever experienced, Cole."

"I told you—"

"I want to stay longer. Not forever or anything. It's just... I-I'm not ready to go."

His eyes widen, and for the first time I see an echo of vulnerability in them. He's like a lost boy who has gotten a present for the first time in his life. Then the pain returns, and he puts back his stern mask.

"It does not matter. I do not want you to stay. No woman will bind me."

I swallow. I know he's just hurt. I know that woman wounded him. I know he'll need time to heal and will resist opening his heart, and I'm patient.

"Not forever, Cole. Just a little longer."

His jaw tightens.

"No."

"You don't have to commit to me. Just be with me a little longer. My pet hotel is taken care of by my employees for a while, and my cats and dogs are with my parents. I want you, Cole."

He shakes his head. "You are not the only one."

That stings. The thought of him with another woman makes me sick. "Okay. I still get one question, don't I? So, here's question number three. What are you afraid of if I stay?"

He turns and strides away, and I follow him.

"Cole! Answer me."

He doesn't respond, just climbs the stairs to the upper deck. I follow, but the ship shakes, and at the same time a sailor runs down the stairs past me. I try stepping to the side but the wet step slips under me. The ship lurches. I stagger back, but instead of hitting the wooden deck, I fall into the darkness.

A scream is ripped from my throat as I flail. Then my back hits the surface of the ocean with a violent blow, knocking the breath out of me. Water floods my ears and my nose and closes above me.

CHAPTER 9

LISA'S SCREAM pierces the air. I turn around, and she is nowhere to be seen. I rush to the railing.

People, the ship, the waves move slowly, as though half frozen in the moonlight. The wind blows, the waves crash against the ship, the men yell, and the sails flap. But my heart is louder, thundering in my ears. My body is rooted to the spot, my blood turning to ice.

Instinct takes over. I cannot leave her behind.

"Man overboard!" I yell. "Drop the anchors!" Then I run down and look around, but I cannot see her. My stomach sinks. Despite the cries of protestation from my crew, I jump into the ocean.

I take a lungful of air. The water seizes me with a sleek resistance and muffles my hearing as I sink. Cool darkness surrounds me. Huge waves pull me down, one after another, without giving me a breath. The ocean is cool and makes my body weightless, and my shirt tickles my skin as I move around. Salt burns my eyes in the dark. I struggle to swim, looking around without seeing anything. Then, finally, I spot long pale limbs struggling in the darkness. I swim to her as she's trying to push herself up to the surface.

I reach her, my lungs already aching from the lack of air. I grab her waist and push her up. I push myself up, too, in long, excruciating strokes. As my lungs begin to burn, my head breaches the water. I gasp and gulp the air like ale.

Lisa is in my arms, her hair in thick wet strands. She is blinking, inhaling hungrily, terrified.

We both move our legs and arms to stay afloat. I hold her close with one arm while working with the other one. "I promised I will not let harm come to you," I whisper to her. "Not while you're mine."

She shakes and trembles in my arms, and I hold tighter. The ship is quite some distance away already, but it is slowing down. The anchor has been thrown out, and soon my team will put down a boat to come and get us. With one arm tight around the most precious thing I've ever held, I slowly make my way towards the ship.

I just hope that saving Lisa will not end up getting us all killed in a battle with the ship that is chasing us.

I must let her go before anything happens. I do not fully believe that she traveled back in time, but I know she believes that. She is pure and honest, and there is not a lying bone in her body. I can feel that.

And if for one mad moment I allow for the possibility that she is right, that time travel exists...

The strange objects from her pockets, the way she talks, her clothes, what she said about her betrothed—all that proves her words.

So.

If she is a time traveler, she will be gone sooner or later. It is better if she leaves before she gets hurt...or killed.

And as I imagine her leaving, my breath catches, and the water presses on all sides like a coffin.

* * *

Lisa

AN ETERNITY LATER, I'm wrapped in the mightiness of Cole's body. We are lying naked on his bed, under the pretense that he needs to warm me up. He's spooning me, his arm and his leg are on top of me, his hot erection pressing against my butt. There's no warmer and safer blanket in the world than his body. We're both under the sheets. Captain Bluebeard is sleeping safely in his covered cage.

I finally stop shaking, Cole's body heat bringing me back to life. The water hadn't been that cold. But the shock and the danger had sent shivers through me.

I feel heavy and tired, as though my whole body is filled with sand. Thinking of the night I've had makes me dizzy. My nerve endings have expanded and I feel sensations like never before. My muscles ache with exhaustion. But despite that, I feel safe. Accepted. Protected.

That connection we had up on the mast is back.

"Do you still want me to go?" I whisper, and turn around to lie on my back and look at his face.

His eyes land on me, dark and warm and haunted.

"Did you really travel back in time?" he asks.

I nod. "I really did. I know it sounds crazy. But if you feel anything at all towards me, if you trust me, if what happened between us means anything to you, please believe me."

His eyes bore into mine, intense, probing, searching. I hold his gaze.

"I believe you, Lisa," he says. "Therefore, you must go."

I let out a shaky breath. He believes me. Which means, there is something between us, and I will not give up.

"You owe me an answer, Cole. What are you afraid of?"

He closes his eyes briefly, as though to calm a distant pain somewhere in his body. His Adam's apple bobs as he swallows, and he inhales sharply. "If you stay a day longer, I will give you the ability to destroy me."

My chest tightens and my throat aches. "What?"

He opens his eyes and looks at me, and there is sadness in their depths. "Because you are a dream come true. A life potion for the dying. A siren that sings so sweetly a sailor doesn't have a choice but follow the song to his death. You will leave me sooner or later. And once you do—"

A tornado of emotion whirls inside of me. It opens my chest and fills my heart with joy and adoration. It's as sweet as the first warm spring day and as beautiful as a canary's song. It reaches all the cells of my body and lights them up like a Christmas tree.

I recognize the feeling and yet I've never felt this before. I was in love with Hank, but the intensity of this is like turning the volume all the way up till the bass vibrates the whole car.

I'm falling in love with Cole.

But I must go. He's right. I don't want to go *now*, but eventually I'll put on the necklace and leave him forever.

Right?

I don't say anything. I have no words. Because what he's saying resonates in my heart like a tuning fork. I'm sinking in his eyes again, in their black, molten danger. I cup his jaw, then reach out and kiss him.

Our lips touch, very lightly, like the touch of butterfly wings. But it sends a rousing wave through my body. Then we come together again, a deeper kiss and yet as soft. Fire begins to sizzle in me, and as his tongue dips into my mouth, I'm lost. I don't belong to myself anymore. I'm his, lost in the power of his gentle hands, melting under the pressure of his powerful body, dissolving in him.

Becoming fully and completely his.

He gently cups my jaw as he continues to worship my mouth. He runs his hand down my body, so lightly it's teasing and igniting me. He cups my breasts gently, and I arch myself into his arms, giving him more access. He growls and puts his mouth on one breast and begins to suck and nip it with his teeth, and then he takes it in hungrily. I jolt and put my hands on both sides of his head. He looks at me.

"Wait," I say. "Not so fast."

"Fast, darling. This is how I want you."

"Please, Cole. If this is the last time—"

I choke on the words, pain gripping my throat. His eyes become clouded with hurt.

"If this is the last time," I say when the emotion settles. "There will be no tying of wrists, no gags, no flogging, or spanking. No rush. Let me make love to you the way I want. To show you how I feel with my body. I want to savor every moment with you."

CHAPTER 10

ole

SHE GLIDES AGAINST ME, and I tighten.

Her way. Show me how she feels about me. What does she mean?

"Show me then," I say.

She kisses me, in those feathery kisses that light even more fire in my blood than full-skin contact.

She shifts to the side and guides me to lie on my back. She kisses me again, and her lips brush mine as though she's enjoying a meal, sweet and tender.

Without stopping the kiss, she climbs on top of me and fondles my chest, spurring my desire and setting my whole body ablaze. She traces her lips down my chin, down my neck, and then down my chest. She continues to my stomach.

She is so beautiful, her still wet hair hanging in long, thick strands. Her skin glows in the dim light of the lamps. Her breasts hang before me, ripe and full and sweet, perfect for my

52

hands. Her thin waist flows into her round hips and the soft curve of her stomach, so seductive. I've had a fair share of my erotic fantasies fulfilled, but this woman—she touches me in ways no one has ever done. She seems to understand me in a way no one could. All women see in me is danger, the man who is not afraid to satisfy them in any way they want. In forbidden ways.

But she satisfies me. In my heart. In my soul.

And she is about to leave. She said it herself—sooner or later, she shall be gone.

And I can *not* bear it. I cannot say goodbye.

She goes on to lick and nip at my stomach, and then down to my throbbing cock. "I want to please you like you pleased me," she says. "I want to send you to the stars like you sent me."

"I am already with stars because I am with you," I murmur.

A sweet smile brightens her face, and she lowers her head and licks the tip of me, sending a jolt of pleasure through me. She takes my head fully in her mouth, and I cannot suppress a low, animal-like growl that escapes my throat. I close my eyes as she pushes my cock deeper into her mouth. Her tongue adds to the sweet torture, and she begins sucking me.

"Oh, Lisa." I hear myself moan. "Yes, like that."

She moans in response and doubles her efforts. I swim in an ocean of bliss, in a sky of burning heat. My erection swells and tightens, and I breathe deeply to stop myself from bursting with pleasure right then and there.

Because I must show her how I feel about her.

"Sweetheart." I raise myself slightly and brush her wet hair out of her eyes. "Come here. I must have you. I must—"

I pull her up gently by the shoulders, and she meets my eyes, as satisfied as a cat after a bowl of cream.

I dip my finger between her sweet folds to make sure she is ready. Her cleft is so sleek with her arousal, I get even harder. I center my erection over her entrance. Her eyes lock with mine, and there's hunger and adoration and something I've never seen before in a woman's eyes…could it be love? My lungs tighten. That can't be right. But I will believe for now, that it is. Inch by inch, I push myself into her.

She meets me with a tight grip of her silky, soft walls, and I groan as she arches her back and moans in response. She begins to move up and down, slowly increasing the pace, grinding against me, and spilling intoxicating pleasure like rum through my veins. It is sweet. It is just her and me. Our eyes are locked, and I gaze into the amber depths of her soul.

I put my hands on her breasts, massaging them, probing her hardened nipples with my fingers, because on some level, I feel this will add to her pleasure right now.

She glides on me, circling her pelvis around my cock.

It is as though we are connected, as though she is a continuation of me and I of her. Like a sea goddess, she is rising and falling with the waves, and I must have her. The thought that she is mine, that her pleasure is mine alone, that I can give to her everything she wants, makes my chest expand with joy.

Her cheeks become flushed, her breathing ragged, and moans of pleasure escape her throat.

I know she is close to her release.

"Oh, Cole," she whispers. "Oh God!"

I thrust into her gently and make circular motions with my hips, and she gasps appreciatively. I increase the speed of my thrusts. Her inner muscles grasp me tighter, and my own pleasure is almost at its peak.

And then I feel her reach the top. She falls apart around me, her insides milking me, and with a deep groan, my own release covers me like a giant wave. I stop seeing anything but her, and she's made of stars. Sweet agony washes through me and around me in wide strokes.

And I know I'm not alone anymore. Because my heart is full with Lisa and always will be.

"Oh, Cole," she whispers as she lies on top of me and breathes heavily. "Oh, Cole."

Our chests rise and fall in one rhythm, and I know I do not want this to stop. I do not want her to go.

But if she wants to go, she needs to do it now. Because I won't bear it if she makes me fall in love with her and then leaves me.

I gently kiss her on the forehead and softly push her to the side. With a heavy heart, my body still washed in the aftermath of our lovemaking, I go to the chest where the necklace with the jade pendant waits.

* * *

Lisa

STILL HOT AND sweaty and pliable, I watch Cole reach the chest, take the keys from his belt laying nearby, and open it. I sit up and cover myself with a sheet, not because I'm self-conscious about my nakedness but because I need protection from the pain of rejection that starts to spread in my heart.

"Cole—"

He reaches in and takes out the necklace. It glistens in the dim light of the room, hanging from his fingers. My arms and legs chill.

He comes to me and holds it out. "Here," he says, his voice hoarse, his eyes dark and intense. "Here's your freedom, Lisa. You fulfilled our agreement. You may go."

I stand up, wrapping the sheet around me. "No. Why don't you believe me when I say I want to stay?"

He closes his eyes for a moment and clenches his jaw. When he looks at me again, they are pure agony. "Because it is not me you fancy. It is the new *you* that you have become."

"What?"

"Like every single woman I've been with, you were looking for an adventure. A thrill. To become bad. And sooner or later, every single one leaves, having taken what they came for."

"No. No. It's different for me. I care about you, Cole. Come on."

"Take it." He shoves the necklace into my hands, and I hold it, shaking. "Put it on. Go on."

I inhale raggedly. Then I raise my head. "Wait, I still have one question left."

He crosses his arms over his chest, and a crease forms between his eyebrows.

"Madame, you are testing my patience. You asked me your last question."

"Which you didn't answer."

He sighs and nods, a pained expression on his face.

I lick my lips. My mouth is dry and warm. My mind is racing. What can I ask him that will make him allow me to stay?

Someone knocks at the door. We turn and see Jenkins peering in. Cole is still naked, and I'm covered in only a sheet.

"Cap'n." Jenkins's face shows concern. "The ship is six miles away. And it changed its flag. It's no Union Jack anymore."

Cole darts to his dresser and shoves dry clothes on.

"Damnation!" he spits out, then rushes towards the door. But before he disappears behind it, he turns to me. His eyes are feverish and burn like two hot coals. He looks at me for a long moment, and there's such pain in his expression it resonates within me and makes my hands shake. Then he breaks eye contact and looks at the jade necklace in my hands. "When I get back, you better not be here."

The door closes behind him with a finality that makes my chest ache.

ole

THROUGH THE SPYGLASS, I can see that this is a frigate. Against the dark sky and the stars, there is an empty void where the flag should be.

Which tells me the flag is black.

A pirate.

A pirate who desperately wants to reach us. And I do not think it is to kiss me on the cheek.

It is likely that blood will be spilled today. And I vow that it will not be my crew's.

But we need to turn to an advantageous position.

The pursuing ship is fast, on full sail, and did not slow down while I was rescuing Lisa.

Jenkins stands next to me. The master gunner, and the ship-master, Bowles, as well.

"It is fast approaching," Jenkins echoes my thoughts.

I glance again in the spyglass. The horizon in front of the

ship is beginning to lighten. By the time our pursuers reach us, the sun will be rising.

"Five miles," I say. "Master Gunner, get the guns ready. Bowles, when they are in shooting distance, we will club haul and give them some iron to chew for breakfast."

We will drop the anchor, turn, and fire. Changing from prey to predator.

"Aye, Cap'n."

"Jenkins, every man must hold a gun or a cutlass."

"Aye, Cap'n."

He leaves to spread the command and prepare the men.

The chaos of the ship preparing for battle whirls around me, but I do not take my eye off the spyglass. And I do not let my thoughts wander to my cabin.

To Lisa.

Did she leave? Is she still there?

My heart splinters with pain, as though a cannonball has hit me in the chest. This is the destiny for me. No woman would love me back, and thinking and hoping otherwise is a mistake. A mistake I learned long ago.

Time crawls, and our pursuers draw ever closer as the sky continues to lighten. With the first sunrays, I can see the ship better, the black flag, and I can even distinguish the people on deck. I strain my eyes to see if I recognize the pirate captain chasing me, but they are still too far.

Soon they are close enough. "Anchors!" I yell, and the ship-master echoes my command.

A loud splash, and the anchors fall fast. "Hold oooon!" I cry, grabbing the nearest cable. The ship careens and turns, and I run to the other side because now we are facing our pursuer's bow, and we can fire right where the frigate is most vulnerable. I take the spyglass and raise my other arm, ready to drop it as the signal to fire.

I look into the glass again—now we are close enough and

there is enough light that I can see the people.

And the sight makes my stomach drop and my mouth open.

On the hull of the ship, hugging the shoulders of a raven-haired woman and waving at me is James.

He beams, waving his arm in wide strokes. The woman next to him is beautiful, and she is smiling, too, a little nervously. James puts his hand to his mouth and shouts something.

"Do not fire!" I cry. "It is Captain James Barrow!"

Surprised outcries run through my crew, and they visibly relax. There will no battle.

My heart drums.

James found a woman? He looks so happy.

My chest squeezes, and my lungs hurt. If James found a wife, a woman to be happy with, I am happy for him. I know how much he longed for it, and how much Anne hurt him.

Just like Duchess Chestwitch hurt me.

And now I have a woman who wants me, too. And I pushed her away, just like Duchess Chestwitch pushed me away.

But what I have experienced with Lisa, the joy of true connection, the joy of companionship, the joy of—love…

I am falling in love with her.

I have avoided risking my heart by immersing myself in physical pleasure.

With Lisa, I found both. A connection of the heart and a connection of the body.

No. I am not ready to let her go. I will have her as long as she will stay. If she wants to stay until tomorrow, she will stay until tomorrow. And I will let her go if she wants to go. It will kill me, but I will not hold her hostage against her will.

I will ask her to stay.

If I am not too late.

I turn and run to my cabin.

The ship, the ocean, the surprised faces of my crew fly by. The breeze pushes against me, as if it wants to stop me.

Finally, the door to the cabin is in front of me, I pass by the front room, and open the door to my bedchamber.

My heart stops. The bed is empty—she is gone.

And then I see her crouched in front of the treasure chest. Putting the necklace back.

She turns around. Her golden eyes burn. Her lips spread in a happy smile.

She flies into my arms, and my whole body expands. *Mine, mine, mine,* drums my heart.

"Mine," I whisper into her silky hair, inhaling the scent of the sun and the sea.

"Yours," she whispers back.

I claim her mouth, her delicious, soft, velvety mouth and sink into it. She responds with the same heat, with the same hunger. A happy eternity later, I lean back.

"You did not go?" I murmur against her mouth. My forehead is pressed against hers, our eyes are locked. Ours souls are, too.

"No, I told you I don't want to. I'm staying. For—longer."

"Good. Because if you didn't, I'd turn the world upside down searching all seas of all worlds for you."

"I still have my last question, Cole."

"You do not, madame."

"Fourth question then. But the most important one."

"What is it?"

"Do…do you think you might fall in love with me?"

My whole being expands. My soul flies high like the victory flag, full like the sails.

"I already am falling in love, my dear. I already am."

She takes my hand in hers. "Good. Because I am, too."

My heart bursts with joy and love and hope—everything I have forbidden myself to feel. Finally, a woman who loves me. Finally, a chance for happiness.

Who knew that this woman would be from the future?

 isa

WATCHING Cole sitting next to me at the dinner table in his cabin does something to me. My legs melt and my veins are filled with laughing gas. His knee touches mine under the table. I inhale his clean smell mixed with the scent of the sea. He devours me with his eyes, his smile sly and a little mischievous. The hair above his ears is gathered in a ponytail, the rest is spread over his massive shoulders.

My man.

Happiness vibrates through every cell of my body. And I can't wait to explore the contents of the kinky chest.

But that I will have to be patient because at the table are Samantha and James. I'm so relieved Samantha is okay, and I'm excited to see her.

It's the evening of the day their ship finally reached us. The ship's cook has made us a celebration dinner, which is intimate in the dim lights of the lamps and feels like a double date.

James flashes a smile to Samantha—a combination of cockiness and shyness.

"Samantha, I told you meeting the right guy would change the way you felt about love," I say.

She rolls her eyes in her mocking way. "You were right, hon. You were right."

I chuckle. She even looks like she belongs in this century. She wears a gorgeous yellow dress—corset and all—with a pale-yellow-flower pattern and a square décolleté trimmed with white lace. Even her hairdo is eighteenth century. James is in a shirt and a blue vest that highlights his tan and his violet eyes, his hair in a short braid.

I'm the only one still wearing modern clothes; although, Samantha gave me one of her dresses. We traveled into the past at the same time, but somehow she has been here for a month while I've only spent one night.

I swing my gaze back to Cole again, and the sight of him takes my breath away. His white shirt is unbuttoned, exposing his tanned chest. I want to run my tongue over his pecs, down his washboard abs, and lower—

Oh God. My face flames. I've never had so many dirty thoughts in my life, especially in front of friends. Cole's eyes burn, never leaving my face.

"And you, too, Cole," James says. "I knew the right woman would come along."

"To women from the future," Cole toasts. We all laugh, raise our glasses of port, and drink.

"Can you imagine," James continues, "that there are no women in our own time who can make us happy? Destiny needed to send them to us from the future. How bad are we, you and I?"

Cole laughs and squeezes James's shoulder. "Quite bad. Quite bad."

"But it wasn't destiny, actually," Samantha says. "James told me it was that man you both knew who owned a pub in Nassau. Adonis, the man with the snake."

"He said something about voodoo," I add. "Maybe he's a voodoo priest or something."

"Whatever the case," Cole says, "he did us a great service. I'll be forever in his debt because he brought Lisa to me."

Our eyes lock, and heat runs between us. My breath quickens, and I want to straddle him right here and now.

"Jeez, get a room, you two." Samantha laughs. "Lisa, I've never seen you like this. Carefree."

She leans closer to the table and locks eyes with Cole, looking suddenly serious.

"You listen, Cole. If you let her get hurt or if you hurt her, I swear to God, I will kill you. I'll find your ass in any Indies, East or West, and I will kick it."

Cole chuckles, his eyelids crawl down, and he looks at me. "The only pain I'm planning to give her is the kind she'll beg me for."

"Oh Lord. TMI, buddy." Samantha throws her cutlery on the plate with a *bang* that wakes Captain Bluebeard. The parrot begins to squawk unhappily.

"Chut. Chut. Chut up."

"Aw, poor fellow, he woke up." I stand and go over to his cage, then lift the sheet.

"Chut up," he repeats.

"His name is Captain Bluebeard," James says. "Cole rescued him."

"Aw, a man who loves animals, Lisa. The man of your dreams," she says.

"Exactly." I return to my seat and cup Cole's jaw.

"And we are most grateful you are taking us to Cuba. Making the passage with friends will be much more pleasant than on Captain Nielson's frigate," James says. "We think it will be easier to buy a villa and a plantation on a big island and get lost among other plantation owners, with me under a new identity. We are going to start a trading company—and Samantha is going to help me run it."

"How did you find us?" Cole asks.

"We ran into Adonis," Samantha says. "He's back in his pub. He told us you were around here, and James hired a ship to try to find you. I was hoping you'd be here, Lisa."

"Samantha, I am your servant," Cole says. "You helped him get the treasure and changed his life. You brought him peace. It is as clear to me as the light of day."

"Oh, Samantha," I say. "This is going to be a great life for you."

"Exactly. I have a man who I love and who makes me happy, and we are going to run a business together and live in the Caribbean! The eighteenth century kicks ass."

Cole leans to James and murmurs, "Do you understand all the words they are saying?"

"Not all, I must admit. But I do enjoy hearing those interesting expressions from the future."

Samantha and I laugh.

"Here's to the four of us." I raise a toast. "To Adonis, who brought us together, to love that crosses time and space, and to the ability to open up and change that makes it all possible."

We clink, with happy smiles, and I kiss Cole while Samantha kisses James.

"Oh, blow the man down, bullies, blow him away," Captain Bluebeard sings. "Way aye blow the man down…"

We all laugh, and I dissolve in the waves of happiness that wash through me. Being with the man I love, seeing my best friend find her own happiness with a wonderful man makes my chest tighten and brings me joy.

I look at Cole and squeeze his hand under the table, and even though it's the only touch we're sharing now, I feel like he knows what I'm thinking and feeling, because that's what I see in his dark eyes.

I lean to him and whisper. "You're the best and the wildest adventure that has ever happened to me. And I look forward to anything life throws at us, as long as it's with you."

"My darling," he whispers back, his eyes burning. "Trust me, the next adventure that awaits you lies in that chest you called kinky…as soon as our dear friends leave us. I promise, you will never be bored with me."

EPILOGUE

hree months later

Lisa

THE SCENT of wood and sea envelops me. The floor sinks under my feet, then rises. Waves splash somewhere nearby.

A man is making deep, animal sounds at the back of his throat. I know that voice. My chest squeezes in a sweet ache.

I sit on the wooden floor, my backpack heavy on my shoulders. The planks under me scratch my fingers and the bare skin of my legs.

Happiness spreads through my stomach.

I know where I am. *Right where I belong.*

I open my eyes and squint into the golden-orange light of the setting sun that falls through a large window.

Cole's window. Cole's cabin. The familiar bed with crumpled sheets, the mirror above it.

The chests with treasure and kinky medieval sex toys.

He's naked and sits in the big chair, which is half turned towards me. He moans and grunts, moving his hand rhythmically up and down. The pungent scent of a man—of sex—fills my nose.

Look at him, how gorgeous he is. His biceps bulging as his arm moves, the muscles on his abdomen straining. His head is tilted back. His long black hair falls over his shoulders.

A piercing pain shoots straight through my chest. How I missed him. The two weeks away in New Jersey, hundreds of years in the future, were torture. I had counted every second. I couldn't be more confident in the rightness of my decision to be with him, no matter the century.

Seeing him like this, just like when I first arrived here, tightens my throat with anticipation and love. Is he thinking of me now? I hope he is.

My skin tingles and my breathing becomes erratic. I put down my backpack, stand on weak legs, and walk to him.

He turns to me, alarmed at first, but then...

Cole watches me with black eyes, naked lust boiling behind them. His gaze travels down my face to my lips, then down my body, and it feels like he's caressing me. "You are a dream come true," he says.

I'm hypnotized, glued to the spot in an all-consuming trance. He's the most powerful man in the world.

He incinerates me with the heat in his eyes. He makes me feel like a goddess.

"You came back," he breathes.

The thought that a man like him is so vulnerable and open to me, loves me, waits for me makes my head spin. I love him, more than anything.

"You didn't think I would?"

"My life would be cursed if you hadn't," he says.

I sink onto my knees between his legs and put both hands on

his thighs. His erection big and heavy, with thick veins, twitches as I look straight at it.

"Anguish for you almost killed me," he says. "You told me you would only be gone a sennight."

"Sorry. It took me longer. But I promised you I'd come back."

"I didn't think you would. I wouldn't blame you."

"I love you, Cole. I would have died over there without you."

He draws in a sharp breath.

"What about your animal inn?" he says.

"I sold it. You're necessary for me to breathe. The pet hotel is not." I burn and melt, and I take a deep breath. "I said goodbye to my family and friends. I'm not going back there. My life is here, with you. If you'll have me."

He closes his eyes for a moment, as though letting the thought sink in and relax him like a drug.

"I'll have you in any way I can." He leans forward, a playful spark in his eyes. "Perhaps I should punish you for taking so long to come back to me."

I draw in a quick breath and suppress a smile of anticipation.

"Punish me?" I whisper, my blood like fire in my veins.

"Oh yes, darling. I want to tie you up so that you'll never leave me again."

He grasps my hands, rises, and I rise with him. He claims my mouth. The kiss is desperate and full of hunger. I moan as he parts my lips. His mouth is soft yet demanding. He sucks my tongue gently, making my muscles and bones liquefy.

By the time he stops the kiss, I'm breathless.

He starts to remove my clothes slowly. First my top, then my shorts, my underwear, and my bra.

My heart slams hard against my rib cage, my insides throb. He goes to his kinky chest and comes back with several short ropes, a long white rope, and a riding crop.

He wraps the long rope around my torso below and above my breasts. From the back, he brings the rope over my shoulder and pulls it under the line of rope below my breasts. He repeats this several times on one side, then switches to the repeat the same process over my other shoulder. The material hugs my flesh, making blood stop in my breasts, leaving them exposed and right there for the taking.

He takes one of the short ropes and attaches it to the longer one, then runs it down my stomach, puts it to the left side of my sex and between my butt cheeks and then hooks it through the rope at my back. Then he runs it to the front again, on the right side, and hooks it to the rope under my breasts. The material presses around my labia, stimulating me in all kinds of ways I've never experienced before.

He makes me sit on the chair.

I gasp softly and let out a calming breath.

"What—"

"Shhh, love," he says.

He takes my arms and ties them to the handles of the chair with short ropes. Every tie is firm and secure, and with every one I feel more and more helpless.

Then he lifts my left leg, bends it, and ties it to my chest. Then he does the same with the right one, completely exposing my most intimate area. He knows every inch of me already, of course, but this is different. I'm helpless.

"Cole…" I whisper.

"Take it in, sweetheart. This is your punishment. This is how I felt when you left. At your mercy."

I hadn't expected this. I'd had no idea this was how me leaving to the twenty-first century had made him feel.

I'm aroused. This isn't exactly comfortable physically, but I don't mind *that*. It's the exposure that brings heat to my cheeks. I'm like a meal on a plate—there for the taking. He can see every inch of me, and every inch is his. He can do what he likes to me, and I can't do a damn thing about it.

This is where our trust comes in.

Even after all the training and every delicious and kinky thing he's done with me over the past couple of months, this is the hottest.

"Tell me how you feel," he demands.

I swallow. "Helpless."

"And?"

"Like I'm yours. Completely, utterly yours."

He nods, his eyes dark, molten onyx slowly take me in. "Good. You are. And I'm yours."

"I brought some presents for you in the backpack."

My bag is heavy with gold and silver I bought with the money I earned from selling everything. But it's also heavy with other treasure.

"Take anything you like," I say.

He walks over and rummages through the backpack, his eyes aflame with curiosity as he removes nipple clamps, handcuffs, Kegel balls—everything I could get my hands on from the modern world that I know he'd appreciate.

He takes a vibrator ring in his hands, one eyebrow arching.

"Press the button," I say.

He raises his eyebrows in question. "What?"

"The little bump on the side."

He examines it and finds the button. With one press of a thumb, it vibrates. He jerks, and curses, but doesn't let the toy out of his hands. I giggle.

"What is this hellish thing?" His eyes are wide on the black silicone ring.

"It's for your pleasure and mine," I say. "You put it on and...well..."

His lips spread in a mischievous smile. "I look forward to exploring your treasures from the future."

He picks up the riding crop that has licked my bottom many times already, and a shiver of pleasant anticipation runs through me.

He approaches me slowly, his magnificent erection swaying.

"Are you ready, sweetheart?" he says as he stands before me. His cock points right at me, and my lips itch to take it in my mouth. "I'm going to welcome you back."

He runs the crop from my neck down my body, stopping at my left breast and slapping it gently. I jerk as a small, electric current of pleasure runs through me. He goes to the second breast and repeats the exercise, making me gasp. The crop trails down my stomach, caressing my skin, and slowly makes its way right to my exposed sex. I clench and shift to lean into the crop as it brushes against my sensitive skin.

A soft slap, and I jerk, gasping for air from the intensity of the pleasure. Then he slaps again. And again. And again.

I make tiny pornographic moans and clench inside. My cleft is hot; my breathing is ragged. He stops and adjusts the rope to apply more pressure around my breasts. The skin on them is already more sensitive, flushed and warm. He leans down and pinches my nipple with one hand, then runs it between his index finger and his thumb while continuing to slap the crop against me. I cry out.

"That's right. Take it in, love," he says.

The slaps get a little stronger, and a shudder runs through my body. I want to take him by the hands and drag him over me, to put his magnificent cock deep inside me, as deep as I can, and have him thrust in and out of me until I can no longer take it.

But I can't. The helplessness is frustrating.

"Do you want to touch me, darling?" he asks as he leans down and gently bites my nipple.

I arch my back, ropes digging into my flesh. They're adding to the sensations already overwhelming me.

"Yes," I breathe out.

"And how does it make you feel that you can't?"

It's so hot.

"I love it."

"Mmmmm." He licks my nipple, sucks on it. His other hand still works the crop and slaps my clit. "Why?"

I gasp with the next slap. "Because I'm yours."

He makes a deep sound of lust in the back of his throat.

"That's right. Mine."

In a lightning-fast move, he withdraws, both his mouth and the crop. He adjusts the ropes around my sex so that they're even tighter, intensifying all sensations there.

He switches on the ring and puts it on his erection. He positions himself on his knees on the floor in front of me, and puts his erection at my hot, wet entrance. It nudges me, stretches me open. The vibration of the ring adds a new edge to my pleasure, and I almost faint as he invades me.

"Mine," he growls.

The wonderful, head-spinning scent of his skin is in my nose. He withdraws and flexes his hips to thrust into me again. He moves slowly, deliberately, but his thrusts are hard.

Possessive.

Needy.

Hungry.

I want to wrap my legs and arms around him, bury my face in his neck. I want to kiss him.

But I can't.

I absorb my vulnerability, and expand, and melt under him. Somehow, my submission makes me stronger. We dissolve and merge together, and his thrusts grow faster, harder.

He's losing control because of me. He loves it as much as I do.

Convulsions begin in my core.

"You're coming," he whispers. "Oh, Lisa, you're…"

And he's right there with me. He's the yang to my yin. I'm his love, his strength, and his weakness. And he's mine.

As we fall apart together, my insides clenching and

unclenching around him, milking him, he cries out my name like it's a prayer, like I'm his religion.

And I scream for him, his name on my lips as I unravel and unwind.

Because with every breath we take together—with every kiss, with every time we make love—I grow stronger, and I know he does, too.

My inner muscles squeeze and burn, and I know that with Cole, I am becoming the person I was meant to be. And it can only get better from here.

THE END

LOVED **the *Called by a Pirate* series?** Travel with me to the Scottish Highlands and read the first instalment of my *Called by a Highlander* series, **Highlander's Captive** now! Scottish time travel romance, plenty of historic details and brawny highlanders. Need I say more?

JOIN THE ROMANCE TIME-TRAVELERS' CLUB!

Join the mailing list on mariahstone.com to receive exclusive bonuses, author insights, release announcements, giveaways and the insider scoop of books on sale - and more!

CALLED BY A HIGHLANDER SERIES (TIME TRAVEL):

Sìneag
Highlander's Captive
Highlander's Secret
Highlander's Heart
Highlander's Love
Highlander's Christmas (novella)
Highlander's Desire
Highlander's Vow
Highlander's Bride
More instalments coming in 2022

JOIN THE ROMANCE TIME-TRAVELERS' CLUB!

CALLED BY A VIKING SERIES (TIME TRAVEL):

One Night with a Viking (prequel)—grab for free!
The Fortress of Time
The Jewel of Time
The Marriage of Time
The Surf of Time
The Tree of Time

CALLED BY A PIRATE SERIES (TIME TRAVEL):

Pirate's Treasure
Pirate's Pleasure

A CHRISTMAS REGENCY ROMANCE:

The Russian Prince's Bride

ENJOY THE BOOK? YOU CAN MAKE A DIFFERENCE!

Please, leave your honest review for the book.
As much as I'd love to, I don't have financial capacity like New York publishers to run ads in the newspaper or put posters in subway.

But I have something much, much more powerful!

Committed and loyal readers

If you enjoyed the book, I'd be so grateful if you could spend five minutes leaving a review on the book's Amazon page.

Thank you very much!

ABOUT THE AUTHOR

When time travel romance writer Mariah Stone isn't busy writing strong modern women falling back through time into the arms of hot Vikings, Highlanders, and pirates, she chases after her toddler and spends romantic nights on North Sea with her husband.

Mariah speaks six languages, loves Outlander, sushi and Thai food, and runs a local writer's group. Subscribe to Mariah's newsletter for a free time travel book today!

facebook.com/mariahstoneauthor
instagram.com/mariahstoneauthor
bookbub.com/authors/mariah-stone
pinterest.com/mariahstoneauthor

9 789083 084237